Kingdom Publishers

Maid for a Purpose

Copyright © Carol Stanley

A catalogue record for this book is available from the British Library.

ISBN: 978-1-913247-30-0

1st Edition by Kingdom Publishers
Kingdom Publishers
London, UK.

You can purchase copies of this book from any leading bookstore or email contact@kingdompublishers.co.uk

PREFACE

After my brother died in 2018, I sat down and wrote an account of my life. Following many troubles, I found healing and peace thanks to God's amazing help. That short book was received well by many who told me what a help and inspiration it had been to them. I decided to enrol for a Creative Writing Course and successfully completed it. Wanting to write a fictional book, I decided to create a story about Naaman's maid. There are only a few lines written about her in the book of Kings in the Bible. Her story is remarkable; God used her to bring healing to a troubled man at great cost to herself. I have given free range to my imagination to create this story basing it on the Biblical facts that we are given. I wanted it to be a happy tale as well as containing sad events. My purpose is to show that out of tragedy and distress hope and joy can come.

God's plans for us are always good and in remarkable ways He works His purposes out if we trust Him. This is what this young girl found. Her faith and trust in her Heavenly Father brought healing to others.

I think this book might appeal to children and teenagers, but I feel that adults will also enjoy the story. It is my first attempt at fiction and is written simply. I trust it will achieve the purpose that caused me to write it.

Carol Stanley

A PORTRAIT OF THE AUTHOR

Carol Stanley is a new author. Her first book "You raise me up" about her spiritual journey with God was well received giving her confidence to write a different sort of book.

She is married to Richard and they live on the South Coast of England. They attend a lively Anglican church and are involved in serving God there. Her hope is that this book will be an inspiration to others, young and old, to trust God in all circumstances of life, believing that He can "work all things together for good" Carol has certainly proved this to be true in her own life.

ACKNOWLEDGEMENT

I would like to thank these people for helping me in writing this book.

My friend Valerie who agreed to proof read the text and suggested corrections.

My husband Richard who took a long time and effort to design the picture for my book cover. His attention to detail has produced a very fine image of the main character Rosa.

And also the friends from Church who encouraged me to write another book.

THANKS TO

Book cover designed by Richard Stanley

CONTENT

CHAPTER ONE

Humble Beginnings

Roza heaved a big sigh and shuddered slightly. She had woken up suddenly with an uneasy feeling that something awful was about to happen. In the darkness she strained her ears for unusual noises, but all was quiet. She was used to the sound of the night insects and an occasional screech owl; cats and dogs were often vocal too. It was footsteps or creaking floorboards that she was hoping not to hear. As she lay there, feeling anxious, her mind wandered back over the events of the last few weeks. Groups of Syrian bandits had been crossing into Israel raiding rural dwellings and destroying crops, also taking livestock. Some shepherds had been killed defending their flocks of sheep and goats. Her parents had forbidden her to wander alone in the fields in case of kidnap.

Roza was thirteen years of age. She was a beautiful girl, the gentle curves of her body beginning to form. Long black hair, deep brown eyes and a smooth olive skin were her main attractions. Clad in her long dresses, with a veil about her head, she was often seen carrying water from the well, feeding the goats and sweeping the courtyard of her house. Her friends envied her slim figure and small features: a curved mouth that always seemed to be smiling; a finely shaped nose; eyes that made many boys hearts melt. She had a quiet manner about her; slightly shy she was always polite but could be quite outspoken if necessary. This sometimes got her into trouble as in her culture females were not encouraged to express opinions, especially in the presence of men. She thought about things a lot and had ideas of what she wanted to do with her life. Once, Roza had spoken out in front of her parents. "Why can't I do all the things that boys do?" she had complained. One look from her father had silenced her.

"Be content with your life girl," he had said sternly. "God has made you a woman so be glad and do not moan!"

It would not be long before her father sought out a suitable husband for Roza; a tingling, weird sensation always filled her whenever she thought of this. Marriage was a mystery to her and not openly talked about at home. A lot of whispering and giggling went on among her friends as they often eyed up the local boys passing on their way to the Chief Elders house for lessons. Girls did not go to school; they were kept at home to do the domestic work until they married and had a home of their own. If they had younger brothers or sisters then they helped look after them so that their mother could go and tend the crops in the fields.

The village that Roza lived in was called Thirza. It was just outside Samaria where the prophet Elisha lived. He was known throughout the land as a man of God who did miracles; people had been healed by him and a widow woman even had her son raised from the dead when she asked Elisha for help. Roza had never seen him but her parents talked of him often.

Her house was a simple brick and clay building. It had two upper rooms, an outside staircase onto the flat roof, then on the lower floor a kitchen, a storeroom, and there was a stable at the back of the building for the animals to be kept in at night. There was a courtyard, and a brick wall around the house. A separate small annexe built on to the house was where her brothers slept. There were shutters around the windows which were closed and bolted each evening. The sturdy door to the house gave security to those inside. There was a place for making a fire in the courtyard. This was often used for cooking the meals.

Thirza was small but set in lovely surroundings. Lush fields were surrounded by high hills, and a river ran alongside the clusters of houses. There was a large meeting place in the centre of the village where worship and communal gatherings took place. Sheep and goats grazed in the further fields, looked after by shepherds who sometimes took their flocks to the hills for better pasture. The main well was outside the village and the flocks were watered there in the evenings. It was also a meeting place for women and girls who came to get water twice a day. They had to wait for the shepherds to lift the heavy stone off the top of the well, then after the sheep and goats had been watered, it was their turn to fill their urns with water for the family.

Tall trees grew around the well; they were good for climbing and the boys were often seen sitting like birds in their branches. When the trees were in blossom displaying fiery red poker type flowers, you could hide in the top of the trees and not be seen. Travellers sometimes rested with their donkeys in the shade provided by the trees, and hospitality was offered them: a bed for the night, or food for their animals.

It was a good place to live, but tension was often felt in the atmosphere as fear of Syrian raids filled the minds of the villagers. War with Syria had been going on for several years. The Chief Elders told them that Israel had broken God's laws and therefore God was not protecting His people anymore. Elisha the prophet had also challenged the King of Israel to call the people to repent of their sins and turn back to God with all their hearts.

Roza's mother was an attractive woman in her thirtieth year. Her former beauty was slightly faded due to her having had five children; hard work had also taken its toll. Roza's father was an elder in the village who spent days talking with other men about the business affairs of Thirza. Her four brothers were aged three, five, seven and nine. Their names were Samuel, Nathan, Matthias and Benjamin. She was the eldest and the only girl. Second mother to the boys, she cared for them when her parents were out working; taking them to school, feeding them, trying to keep them well behaved, all a difficult task at times. It left little time for herself, but she accepted her part in the family, as her father had instructed her to. It was the custom in Israel.

Roza's family loved God and tried to obey Him in their way of life. Daily prayers were said at home and the Jewish festivals observed regularly.

The Passover was one of the main events in the village. Once a year every home remembered the escape by their forefathers from Egypt where they had been slaves. They had been promised a land flowing with milk and honey, God's chosen place for them. A lamb was cooked and eaten and a special ceremony was acted out. There were other special times of celebration all to remember God's goodness to the nation of Israel.

Roza felt God close to her at all times and talked to Him as she went about her chores. She knew all the stories about her ancestors: Abraham, who was called by God to leave his country and go to the land of Canaan. He had a son in his old age called Isaac. God was starting to build a people who would follow Him. Moses, how he had led the children of Israel across the Red sea to safety; David the shepherd king who had defeated the giant Goliath in his youth, and many other people who followed God and trusted Him to help them through hard times. It made Roza feel that she too could trust God to keep her safe.

CHAPTER **TWO**

Friendship and Fear

Morning broke on a perfect day. Roza had slept through uneasy hours, her dreams forgotten now. She washed herself and went downstairs to where her mother was making breakfast. The boys were running around and making a lot of noise. Her father had left early for a meeting and would not return until evening.

"Boys come and sit down to eat," her mother commanded, and they obeyed her. Roza went outside to do her chores first. Passing by the house was her friend Daniel.

"Hello Roza," he called. She smiled at him. He was also thirteen, tall with a good appearance. Black hair, brown eyes with long eyelashes, a sturdy frame. His striped coat was red and brown, his legs suntanned and his sandals laced up with goats skin.

"Where are you going Daniel?" she asked.

"To spend the day looking after the flocks; my brother is not well, so I have to do it. Will you come and see me at high noon and bring me some food please?" he pleaded. Roza shook her head.

"I am not allowed to wander in the fields alone: it is too dangerous."

"Oh, I am sure you will be alright, it is not too far to walk before you get to me," insisted Daniel. "I will look out for you and watch for any trouble." It was a really tempting thought for Roza; to spend time with Daniel who she really liked. If there was anyone that she wanted to marry it was him. Her mother would be in the fields and father out all day, the boys at school. Why not? She was sure it would be quiet and the walk would be good.

"I will see," she said.

"I would love to spend time with you," Daniel looked at her wistfully, "I get bored sitting with the flocks on my own."

Later on, returning from taking the boys to the meeting place, and saying "Goodbye" to her mother, Roza packed up some food in a basket, did the rest of her work and considered her plan. If she took the path beside the river there might be people around so it would be safe. In a way it was disobeying her parents, but Daniel needed company and she was sure God would look after her. She would wait until the sun was high, wrap herself in a shawl so that no one would recognize her easily, and slip off to meet Daniel. It was hot when she left. Excitement filled her. It was an adventure which she felt would make her life a bit more interesting; wait till she told her girl friends about it! The river was sparkling and women were washing their clothes on the banks. She walked quickly past them, not stopping to talk. As she looked at the river, childhood memories came flooding in of days when the boys had gone swimming there in the summer. The village girls had hidden behind the bushes watching their antics with jealousy. If they had been discovered, it would have meant a whipping for them!

The distant fields were very green, and the blue hills behind them soft with shadows. As she went on it became a more solitary walk and slight feelings of nervousness came over her. She pushed them away. It was not too far to the grazing lands where Daniel would be. There was a small forest on her right hand side now; it looked dark like a gaping mouth. Birds twittered from the depths and the wind rustled the leaves of the trees. Although she was familiar with this forest, today it gave her a feeling of fear. Anything could be hiding amongst the old gnarled trunks of the trees. She shuddered as she had in the night time. Pressing on, she soon reached more open country and in the distance, like a speck of dust, she saw a figure. That must be Daniel. Running now, she felt the wind whip across her face and a sense of exhilaration filled her. She could not wait to see Daniel and spend time with him. It took her half an hour to reach him and there he was sitting on a rock surrounded by grazing sheep and goats.

"Roza," he said, "You came!"

"Yes," she puffed. "I brought you some lunch and a flask of grape wine." They sat together, two young friends becoming close in their feelings for each other. They had known each other since childhood; they had a lot in common.

"I want to move the flocks a bit nearer to the hills," said Daniel. Roza looked worried.

"I can't go too far away from home," she said." I have to get back to fetch the boys from school at four o'clock."

Daniel smiled. "There is plenty of time Roza; it is not high noon yet!"

She smiled back. "Alright, let's go now and make the most of the day." They stood up and Daniel, going ahead of the flocks, called them in the special way that the sheep and goats knew and responded to. Roza followed, taking her shawl off as the air grew warmer and lifting her face to the sun. "Thank You God for getting me safely here," she prayed. A twinge of guilt rose up in her heart. She knew that she was not supposed to be here really.

It was about midday when they sat down to eat. All was quiet except for the noise of the sheep bleating and the wind rustling in the grass. Then, in the distance they heard a rumbling sort of thumping sound, and a cloud of dust appeared far away.

"What is that?" asked Roza.

"I don't know," replied Daniel frowning and squinting as he looked at the approaching dust storm.

They stood up and gazed at the unfolding scene. As they stared, a fast moving group of black clad riders appeared. They were riding horses. In their hands were whips which they used to make the horses run faster. Spears strapped to their backs glinted in the light.

Suddenly Daniel shouted. "Roza I think it is a raid!"

"Raid," she screamed, "What do you mean?"

"The Syrians are coming!" Daniel turned to her. "Run Roza, run and hide!"

"I can't leave you!" screamed Roza.

"Just do as I say," he demanded. She turned and fled as fast as she could back towards the forest. That was the only cover she could think of although it terrified her to go into that dark place. Looking back she saw that Daniel was going to sound his ram's horn as a warning to the village. Then a terrible sight met her eyes.

The horsemen were almost on him. One of them got to Daniel and knocked him over so that the horn fell out of his hand; he fell crumpled to the ground. "Daniel!" she screamed and then instantly regretted it.

The men looked in her direction, and she began to run again. Her legs felt like jelly. "Faster!" she gasped to herself. "God help me." A loud noise behind her made her yell in terror. Suddenly strong overpowering hands grabbed her and she was lifted off the ground. A cloth was placed over her eyes and mouth; she was sitting on a horse, the man behind her holding her tightly against him. She struggled. A cuff on her head dazed her and she fainted.

CHAPTER **THREE**

Terror and Travel to the Unknown

When Roza came round, she realised that she was tied to one of the trees by the well, lying with hands and feet bound tightly. Looking around she saw that other people were also captive, mostly women. She knew a lot of them by sight but not name. In the distance she could hear shouts and the sound of a battle going on. "The boys!" she gasped. "My mother and father!" A sense of terror came over her as she wondered if they were still alive or also captured. She could not talk to anyone else as her mouth was gagged with a cloth. After a while everything went quiet and then towards them came the Syrian bandits running as if being chased. They untied the captives and put them all, including her, into a big wagon, covered, and drawn by two horses. Off they went at breakneck speed towards the Syrian border.

Horror seized Roza. She was being taken away from home to a strange land, her future unknown. She prayed earnestly:"Lord God of Abraham, Isaac and Jacob, help me and keep me safe in Your arms." She realised that this was all her fault. If she hadn't disobeyed her parents and gone wandering off to meet Daniel, this might never have happened to her. "Forgive me," she prayed. "I have sinned against You and my family." All at once a feeling of peace came over her and a verse from the Psalms of David came into her mind that they often sang in the worship gatherings. "He will cover thee with His feathers, and under His wings you will trust." It was as if God was saying: "I know what has happened to you and I am with you." She fell asleep from sheer shock and exhaustion.

When she woke, it was very dark and the wagon was still. The flap at the end was opened and a man climbed in amongst them. He untied them, pushed them out of the wagon into a tent that had been erected. There he tied their feet up again but left their mouths and hands unbound. Food was then placed in front of them; bread and a sort of soup. Water in a jug plus cups came in too. Roza was very hungry and so took some bread and soup. The other women were more cautious.

"I don't trust these brutes," said one woman.

"Oh don't worry," said another. "They won't hurt us; they want us as slaves, for money. It is in their interest to keep us alive and in good condition." In silence each woman ate and drank. Everyone was so shocked and frightened that not much was said.

"You will be alright," one of them said to Roza. "You are too young to be sold as a wife, not like us. We have no choice."

"What will happen to me?" asked Roza.

"Probably you will be bought by a family who need a maid to do the work in their house and serve the meals." The woman looked vaguely familiar to her. It was all very scary. Eventually they all went to sleep.

Roza dreamt of her childhood. After the disappointment of their firstborn being a girl, her parents had loved her. They had given her everything they could to make her happy. She was taught the Holy Scriptures, and the stories of how her ancestors had walked with God enthralled her. The nation of Israel came into being through Jacob; his twelve sons became the founders of twelve tribes after their escape from Egypt. Moses had led them out into the desert where they travelled to the Promised Land. Disobedience caused forty years of wandering before the next generation entered the land. They fought and conquered, settling into their own territories. She had a great sense of belonging to God's people. Life had been good, and when her brothers were born, she became the one who helped care for them. The meeting place in the centre of the village was very important to all. Every week they attended the service there and the Torah was read and worship observed. The Elders kept an eye on the villagers spiritual lives, bringing discipline where needed and collecting the tithes from the people required by the Biblical law. On the Sabbath they rested and no work was done. She used that day to read books and write her thoughts down. She was learning fast about life and her faith.

A shove in the leg woke her. A big cistern of water had been placed before them for washing in.

"We have to get clean so that we look good for the slave market," said one of the women. Their legs were untied and each person had a quick wash with a cloth provided. It was enough just to get the dust and grime off their skin.

Then bread and cheese was given to them. They were bundled

back into the wagon and tied up again. There was no point in trying to escape; the bandits were watching their every move.

Roza thought of her family and Daniel. What had become of them? She wondered if they were all dead. She had seen Daniel fall to the ground. Her village had been in chaos but her parents had been away in the fields and at meetings. Perhaps they were alright. However, the boys had been in the village school. As she thought about them she began to weep big tears of grief. A woman next to her put her arms around her.

"Try not to be distressed," she said, "It will not help you; trust in God and ask Him to be with you and your family."

Roza looked up. "It was my fault," she wailed. "I was supposed to be looking after the boys and our home, but I wandered off into the fields."

"It is too late to torture yourself now," said the woman. "What is done is done."

CHAPTER **FOUR**

Sold Into Slavery

After a while, the wagon stopped. There was a lot of noise outside; sounds of donkeys' hooves and people talking. They were told to get out and what confronted them was a chaotic scene. Horses and cattle were being ridden or driven along. Market stalls and brightly coloured baskets were everywhere. People argued, laughed, and chatted all around the area; they seemed to be excited about something. There was a huge open square with fences around it and it was to this place that they were herded. In the background were tall buildings with many windows in them. Out of these people were hanging, looking down at the square. Roza and the other women were chained to the fences: this was the Slave Market. It was terrifying! Suddenly a loud horn sounded. From somewhere scores of men and official looking people appeared. Each woman was examined and talked about. They were prodded and made to turn round, like animals. Then it seemed as if bargaining and arguments started; the price was being fixed for the sale of each woman.

Roza was left for a while. She was shaking from head to foot. She looked up and saw a man in some sort of uniform watching her. He had a rather gentle face but there was something not quite right about his skin. It was pitted and red; his neck was covered in what looked like blisters. Otherwise he was handsome. On his hands were more scars and spots. He looked important.

She couldn't take her eyes off him. He approached her. She shrank back. His smile made her feel less afraid. He turned to one of the officials. In a language that she did not understand, he communicated with the man. A conversation went on for a while; then it seemed to finish with satisfaction on both sides.

"Come with me." The man spoke to Rosa in Aramaic which she understood. Roza did not think she had a choice, she was a slave, captured by enemies. He unchained her and she followed him to a carriage drawn by two magnificent Arab horses. "Sit beside me," he said.

Roza got in and the journey began. It was obviously a city that they were in; could it be Damascus the capital of Syria? She saw many houses and roads.

After a few miles, plots of land and farm buildings appeared. A wide river ran alongside the road; in the distance huge mountains towered over the land. To Roza they seemed like giants; she could imagine them suddenly walking and trampling everything under foot. This was how she felt at the moment: afraid of everything.

It took half a day to get to the man's property. As they got nearer, she saw a huge house in the distance. It was white with a large area of land in front of it. To the side she noticed what appeared to be stables as well as several smaller buildings also white. She imagined that at the back of the house there would be gardens and plots to grow crops in. She shivered. What was her future to be like here? So far she had been treated gently and not prodded and poked like the other poor women. She looked up at the man beside her. What would he be like; did he have a wife or children? She offered a prayer to God: "Please be with me and help me to behave in the way that You want me to in this place. May I always keep my faith in You."

On arrival at the house, Roza sat still and waited. The house had a great door with an arch over it; steps made of marble went up to the entrance. White ornate fences surrounded the house. The windows were wide and each one had an iron parapet outside of it. The flat roof seemed to have a garden growing on it. Grass hung over the roof and flowers in pots made a colourful display. There seemed to be a few seats scattered around. Statues stood around in the courtyard where they had stopped.

"Get out now," said the man. He helped her down, his hands strong but not hurting her. The door opened and on the steps stood a very beautiful looking woman. She was not tall, but stately. Her black hair was plaited and wound around her head. Entwined in her hair were jewels. Gold hoops hung from her ears.

Her skin was pure and olive in colour and her eyes were heavily made up with black round them. She wore a long robe tied round the waist with a gorgeous sash of gold. The colour of the robe was purple with blue flowers sewn on to it. Roza had never seen one like it before.

A necklace of emeralds adorned her neck, flashing in the sun, and rings on her fingers sparkled. Her feet were encased in white sandals, very elegant.

"This is your mistress, my wife," said the man. "You will be serving her in the house." They walked toward her, Roza trembling with fear. Just as the man had gazed at her, this woman's eyes fixed on Roza as if she was absorbing every detail of her appearance.

"How old are you child?" she asked, also speaking in Aramaic.

"Thirteen, my lady," answered Roza. She did not know what to call her mistress. The woman opened the door wider and beckoned for Roza to follow her inside. "I am entering a new life and leaving all I have known behind," thought Roza to herself. She took her first steps into the unknown.

CHAPTER FIVE

Daniel's Trials and Escape from Death

Daniel lay still. His head was throbbing after being felled to the ground. Temporary unconsciousness had come over him; when he came to he heard the bandits still around him. Roza's screams haunted him. What had happened to her? He decided to hold his breath and pretend to be dead. He was good at this. Swimming under water in the river, competing with his friends to see who could stay down the longest had expanded his lungs. A man stood over him and poked at his body with a spear. Holding his breath Daniel prayed hard. After a while the bandits rode off, leaving him lying there in the dirt. He dared not move. Time passed and eventually he stood up and looked around. Horrified, he saw that part of the village was on fire. Figures were running around, the scene was chaotic. Faint screams could be heard. Daniel ran to the wood and crept in to the dark interior. He would hide here until all was quiet in Thirza.

As darkness fell, he dared to approach the well outside the village. There were ropes lying discarded on the ground and he could see tracks in the sand that looked like wheel marks. The fires were still burning in the centre of Thirza and he ran toward the blaze. Shock filled him as he realized that his own house was destroyed. Where were his parents? Just then figures appeared from the area of the meeting house. The chief elder was hurrying along with the youngest boys following him.

Running up to them he asked: "Where are my parents, where is Roza?"

"Your father has been killed, Daniel, but your mother is safe with us. She managed to hide; your older brothers are captured." The Elder put his arm round Daniel's shoulders. He led him to a nearby house where people were gathering. Amongst them was his mother.

"Daniel, where were you?" she screamed at him.

"Out in the country mother," he replied. "They knocked me out and I pretended to be dead. Where is Roza?"

"She has been captured and taken away to Syria," his mother wept. Daniel gave way to sobs. His father was dead. His best friend was captured and his older brothers too. It was too much to bear. He found out all the details of what had taken place: the men who had been killed defending the village, the women taken away. That night nobody slept. They all huddled together numb with disbelief at what had occurred. Daylight revealed the whole ghastly scene.

"We must rebuild and fortify our walls," the Elders commanded. Everyone got to work and over the next few months houses were rebuilt, walls repaired and life somehow returned to normality. Deep wounds of loss affected many, especially Daniel.

He was devastated that he had not protected Roza and his family. Guilt tore through him and his nights were tormented with nightmares. One day he went into the meeting house and shouted at God.

"Why did you allow this to happen," he yelled. No one else was there or so he thought. Then a man came up to him. It was one of the elders, named Asher.

"God never makes mistakes Daniel," he said.

"Well he did this time!" Daniel's face was contorted with rage.

"If you let bitterness and anger fill your heart my son, it will destroy you." Asher took his hand. "God is bigger than all our troubles. Give all your hurt and misery to Him. Ask for peace and that you will be able to accept His will." He left Daniel. Kneeling down, Daniel let himself cry hot tears for a long time. It felt as if he was being washed inside and at last he felt peace pervading him.

"My Father, help me to carry on and grow into a man that trusts God," he prayed. "I do not understand why this has happened but my life belongs to You. Do with me as You will." Getting up he walked out into the sunshine and let his tears dry. "Bring Roza back to me please," he pleaded. He turned toward his new house where his remaining family lived. "I will look after them and be the head of the house." Straightening himself with new resolve in his heart he went in to his mother.

CHAPTER **SIX**

A Grand House and A Slave's Life

s Roza followed her new mistress through the door, her heart was beating fast. She had no idea what to expect; Syrian houses were unknown to her.

The interior of the house was very grand. There were stone tiled floors and pictures hanging on the walls; an ornate staircase leading to the upper floor; large urns filled with flowers; doors of oak behind which must be rooms. There were also stairs going down to a lower floor.

"You will sleep down here," said the woman leading the way. Roza was shown a small room with a simple mattress on the floor covered by a blanket of red material. There was a jug and bowl for washing on a low table, and a small stool. It had a window looking on to the courtyard. Going upstairs again, she was shown a kitchen area where other woman servants were preparing food.

"You will do work here and serve the meals," she was told. "You must wait on me and do exactly what I tell you." Roza bowed meekly.

"You are forbidden to talk to any of the men, especially my husband, but you can talk to me and the other women," was the next commandment.

"Please, what do I call you?" asked Roza timidly.

The woman smiled."Call me Ba'alah," she said. "That is Mistress in my language. I will show you how to look at my hands with which I will signal to you what to do."

Roza bowed again. Her mistress took her to the servants' area and beckoned to a woman who was fairly elderly.

"Take this girl and give her a good wash," she said. "In the chest in the hall there are clothes. Select some suitable ones for her and then give her something to eat." Turning to Roza she said: "When you have eaten, come and find me in the room with the purple hanging over the door." With a swish of her clothes she departed.

The elderly woman led Roza to a small room upstairs, fetched a large stone bath, and left her while she went to get water for her wash. Returning with another woman, they both upturned their large urns into the bath.

"Get in," she was told. Shyly Roza removed her dirty clothes and stepped into the bath. The water was warm and she relaxed as it soaked into her skin. The two women gave her a sponge and soap with which she scrubbed herself; she also put her head under the water and washed her matted hair. Getting out she was dried, a dress was found that fitted her and sandals too were placed on her feet.

"This dress belonged to the last maid," said the elderly woman. "She got too friendly with the men so watch out!" Back to the kitchen they went where Roza was given bread, olives and cheese plus a drink. "You had better go to the mistress now; remember to call her Ba'alah," smiled the elderly woman who's name Roza had not been told.

Finding the room with the purple hanging was easy. She knocked and was told to enter. In the room she saw her mistress sitting in a chair by the window. At her feet was a stool.

"Sit here," the woman said.

"Yes Ba'alah," whispered Roza.

"What is your name child?" her mistress asked.

"Roza, Ba'alah," she answered

"You are probably sad and frightened. Unfortunately you are the spoils of a long running war between us, Syria, and Israel. Do you have family?"

Roza tried not to weep. "Mother and Father and three brothers; I do not know now if they are dead or alive," she said faintly.

"You must not show any feelings here," her mistress said. "You belong to us now and I expect you to wait on me as I instruct you."

Over the next hour, she taught Roza the hand signals that would tell her what to do. These signals were to save conversation. A wave of the hand toward the door was Roza's dismissal. Tapping her shoulders meant that she wanted her shawl. Pointing to her mouth meant that she required food or drink. A finger toward the stool was a command for Roza to sit. Otherwise she spoke her orders. Roza's duties would be dressing her Ba'alah each day, serving all meals, cleaning the house and helping in the kitchen. One afternoon a week, she could rest and walk round the gardens speaking only to women.

Roza was fighting a losing battle with her eyes. They were

drooping because she was exhausted.

"You are tired," the Ba'alah said. "Go to bed, but at dawn you will be woken. Wash and come straight to my room upstairs. It has a screen of goat's hair outside."

"Yes Ba'alah," said Roza. She got up and went to her room, took off her dress and lay down under the blanket. She had no idea what time it was, but darkness was descending outside her window and the first stars appearing. Her tears started, and softly through them she prayed, "My God, I give You my life. Be with me and help me to serve these people with love not hatred. If my family are alive be with them and let them not forget me." Sleep overtook her and she had a dreamless night.

Light filtering through the window woke her. For a moment she had no idea where she was. The door opened and she sat up in fright.

"Wash quickly and go to your mistress," a voice commanded. Jumping out of bed, Roza saw water in the jug on the small table. She poured it into the bowl, splashed water over herself quickly, put on her dress, tidied her hair with the comb that had been left for her, and rushed upstairs. The room with the goats hair screen was the first door on the corridor.

"I am here Ba'alah," she called.

"Come in child," she heard. The mistress was in a large ornate bed which had blue sheets and an embroidered covering. Her room was very large and there were some beautiful tables and chairs under the large windows. Flowers were in abundance in decorated urns. Pictures hung on the walls. Several of them were of people: men, women, girls and boys all looking very serious. Ornate tall cupboards stood against the walls.

"Bring me my robe." She pointed to a robe hanging over a chair.

Roza fetched it and helped her mistress up into the chair. "Water is in that urn. Pour it into that bowl and wash my face and hands," was the order. Roza did this pretty well. "Now dress me with the clothes that are in that chest." All this accomplished, her mistress told her to go to the kitchen and prepare her breakfast. "Bring it into the same room as yesterday Roza," she ordered. This was the first time Roza had been called by her name in this house. Off she went where the food was waiting for her to make breakfast. It was goat's milk, eggs, bread, cheese and honey.

"Put it all on that silver tray," she was told, "Don't drop it!" She managed to negotiate the tapestry door and laid the tray on a table in front of her mistress who was sitting in the chair by the window. She was ordered to sit on the stool and watch the hands for signals. After a few mistakes, which were tolerated, she got more familiar with these. The rest of the day consisted of sweeping the courtyard and rooms, serving the meals, and learning basic cooking. The other women were quite friendly and she felt less afraid. In the distance she occasionally heard marching and horses plus shouts. She presumed it came from the soldiers who she had observed outside the window clothed in matching tunics with swords round their waists. She did not dare ask any questions of anyone. As she was coming out of the mistress's room that evening, the front door opened, and the master entered. Roza quickly ran into the kitchen. "The master has come," she told the other servants.

"His name is Naaman," she was told." He is a great man. He commands the army of Syria and has won many victories in the war with Israel. The king honours him greatly; they meet with each other and talk often. He is not cruel like other soldiers, but treats us all kindly."

Roza plucked up courage and asked," What is wrong with his

skin?" The servants looked at each other.

"He has a form of leprosy Roza. It is not as bad as it could be but he has to sleep separately from the mistress and they cannot have children because of it." As Roza was new to the house, she did not like to ask any more questions.

She was not called to sit with her mistress that evening, so the elderly lady who she learned was called Sarah taught her how to repair clothes. That night in her prayers she asked God to help Naaman get better as she felt sorry for him. "The prophet Elisha who lives near Thirza would be able to heal him. He is so far away though." She tried not to think of home.

Sleep overtook her, and in her dreams she saw Naaman running away and the mistress crying in her tapestry room.

CHAPTER SEVEN

A Lonely Mistress- Roza's Courage

The days passed and Roza became used to the routine of serving, cleaning and cooking. She got to know the other servants. Other than those in the house there were women who tended the gardens; she saw men working on the crops further afield. The young woman who worked in the garden was called Hannah. She told Roza of her own capture a few years previously.

"I was alone in the fields tending the crops. The bandits came and snatched me away. My family were slaughtered in the raid; I saw it with my own eyes. I hate being here." Roza felt so sorry for her.

"God has been with me," she told Hannah.

"I do not believe in any God!" spat Hannah. Her bitterness made Roza afraid to say any more.

The head servant in the house was Sarah, the elderly lady. Under her was Deborah, the cook, and then Lydia who was in charge of buying all the household supplies. Roza talked to them sometimes of her faith in God; they listened and she felt that they liked to hear her sharing the stories of her ancestors in Israel. She was puzzled that Naaman did not come to the house too often. Her concept of marriage was that a man and a woman lived together and shared all their lives. Then she remembered his leprosy. Sarah had told her that this disease could be passed on to another person if there was too much contact. Her heart grieved for the lost relationship between her mistress and Naaman.

On her afternoons off she was allowed in the gardens. They were full of flowers, statues and olive trees. Seats of stone were placed under the trees and she used to sit on one of these. A few months after her capture, she was sitting in the garden one afternoon. "I would like to sing," she mused. Then a verse from the Psalms came into her mind. "By the rivers of Babylon, there we sat down; yea we wept when we remembered Zion. How shall we sing the Lord's song in a foreign land?" Tears came as Roza thought of her family and Daniel. "I will sing," she said defiantly. "I am quite happy here and have been treated kindly." Opening her mouth she began to sing a song that she had learned as a child; a haunting chant but with beautiful words. Suddenly behind her she heard movement. Spinning round, she saw her mistress standing near to her. Jumping up, she bowed.

"What were you chanting child?" she was asked.

"An old song from my childhood days, Ba'alah," replied Roza. The mistress sat on the seat and beckoned for Roza to join her. Timidly she did.

"I have noticed that you are peaceful and very obedient," the mistress remarked. "Why is that?" Roza swallowed and prayed silently.

"I believe in the God Who made heaven and earth; He is helping me," she whispered.

"What is His name?" she was asked.

"His Name is so holy that we do not say it. He is great and mighty. Our nation was created when He called Abraham, my forefather, to follow Him into the land of Canaan. Many miracles and wonderful events happened. He is good and loves those who do His will." Silence reigned for a while.

"I have heard of this God," said her Ba'alah. "There was a story."She wrapped her robe more tightly around her. "It was when the army of Moab went to attack Israel. They got up in the morning and saw water looking as if it was full of blood. Thinking the Israelites were dead, they went to plunder them. However, it was a mirage. When they got there, the Israelites were very much alive and chased them, defeating them soundly. It was said that their God made that happen." She looked at Roza. "Have you heard that story?" she asked.

"I think so," said Roza. "There are so many like that." Shifting her position, she said shyly:" If only my master could go to see the Prophet Elisha, he could be healed of his leprosy." The mistress's eyes widened.

"Who told you about that?" she demanded. Roza felt fear rising in her. She did not want to get into trouble or betray anyone else either.

Having been brought up to always speak the truth she whispered,

"It was my fault; I asked. They were not sure whether to tell me, but did. I felt sorry for the master." After what seemed like an eternity, the mistress smiled.

"I am glad that you care," she said. "Roza I am very unhappy. When we were married all was wonderful. I wanted children but a few months after we came here, my husband became ill with leprosy. He caught it from a prisoner who was brought back from Israel. It is not the worst kind, but we cannot be together fully as a married couple; children are out of the question. I might catch it if we were too close." She sighed deeply. Roza was touched and amazed that her Ba'alah was confiding in her; such intimate details which were nothing to do with her.

"Elisha the man of God does miracles," she told her mistress shyly. "There was a great woman in a place called Shunem. Elisha used to pass her house often, and one day she and her husband built a little room for him to stay in on their roof. He used it a lot. To show his gratitude he promised her that she would bear a child; she had none. It happened and she had a son. However the boy became ill and died. Heartbroken, she ran and told Elisha. They laid the boy in Elisha's upper room. The prophet shut himself in with the boy and prayed to God even though the lad was dead. After a while, sneezing could be heard; rushing upstairs the woman saw her son sitting up. He was alive!" She looked at her mistress. Tears were coursing down her face. "Many other miracles like that happened," Roza said. "I am sure my master could have one too if he went to see the prophet."

Getting up, her mistress walked away without another word and Roza was left alone. "Lord God, help my master to be told about the Prophet and save me from trouble." she prayed. Her heart was beating fast. Had she been too forward in what she had told her Ba'alah? Could God have sent her here for a purpose? She was shaking and feeling cold so she went into the house and sat down on her bed. After a few minutes sleep came over her. It was dark when she awoke, and a figure was standing by her. Frightened, she sat up.

"The mistress wants you to come to her room, "a voice which she recognised said. It was the elderly servant. Quickly Roza washed her face and went to her mistress. Opening the door, she was shocked to see both her mistress and her master there.

"Now I am to be sent away," was her thought.

"Roza, tell your master what we shared in the garden," commanded her Ba'alah. "You can speak to him when I am here." Haltingly, Roza told the story again about Elisha and the miracles he had done in the Name of God. Naaman, the tall, gentle commander of armies, questioned her at length making sure that he knew all the facts.

"Do you really think this man can help me?" he asked.

"Yes master, I am sure he would help if you went and asked him," replied Roza. "He loves God and I believe God wants to help everyone who is in trouble." She waited for a response.

" Israel and Syria have been enemies though," said Naaman.

Roza screwed up her face in the intensity of her thoughts. She was only thirteen. "Elisha does not always take sides in war, I think," she whispered. "He does what God tells him to do."

"So he would welcome me?" asked Naaman.

"I am sure he would," Roza responded. "Perhaps it would be good to ask the king of Israel if you could visit the Prophet in case your arrival is seen as a threat." This wisdom was unusual in a girl of thirteen, but God was helping Roza.

"I will have to get permission from my king too," Naaman said. "He has authority to allow me to go, or he may object."

Roza was told to go and get food then go to her bed. As she

dismissed her, the Ba'alah took Roza's hands in hers.

"Come to me early tomorrow as usual," she said.

Exhausted with all the emotions that had flown through her body, Roza could hardly eat. When her head touched her bed, she was unconscious immediately. Her dreams were full of images: Horses, soldiers, her mistress crying, Naaman going on a journey somewhere. "Where is he going?" voices called. Darkness took him out of her sight.

She dreamt no more and the light woke her. It was time to get up and start her duties. "What will happen today?" she wondered. She said her prayers and got washed. "It is all in Your hands Father God," she whispered.

Life was taking unexpected turns for Roza. Her mistress was ready for her. Nothing more was said about the conversations of the previous day; the time passed in the usual way. Roza realised that it was her birthday and she had reached the age of fourteen. She did not mention it to anyone but remembered how she would have been treated at home. There would have been a special breakfast of yoghurt and honey, followed by gifts and lots of friends arriving. The thought made her terribly homesick. Daniel was in her thoughts a lot that day. Was he still alive? She loved him and longed to see him again. However, she was fairly happy here in this foreign place; her mistress treated her almost like a daughter. God had kept her and maybe it was all for a reason. Also remembering her mother, father and brothers, Roza surrendered them all into the will of God who she knew loved them and did not make mistakes. In her bedroom, which had no curtains, the moon shone brightly through the window bathing her in light. "May Your light shine on all those that I love," she whispered. With her emotions in turmoil she slept.

CHAPTER **EIGHT**

Naaman's Journey Begins

Roza woke up with a start. Loud noises and tramping hooves outside her window made her jump up to see what was happening. A large group of men were assembling. They were loading a carriage with what looked like clothes and bags of money. As she watched, Naaman rode up on his horse; the mistress appeared already dressed. It was only just dawn. Roza washed and dressed, went to the kitchen and started to prepare the breakfast for her Ba'alah.

"They are going on a long journey," Sarah the elderly servant told her.

"Where?" asked Roza. Sarah would not tell her anymore.

"Go to the mistress and serve her breakfast," she ordered Roza. Entering the tapestry room, Roza saw that the mistress was staring out of the window. Roza placed the tray on the table and stood ready to serve.

"You have started something my child," said her mistress. "Your master has gone to see the Prophet in Israel. He had an audience with the king and told him all that you said about Elisha healing people. So the king has written a letter to King Joram of Israel asking him to receive my husband and help him to be healed of his leprosy."

Roza's mouth fell open. Shock flooded her. This was soon replaced with a great sense of excitement. They had believed her! So much so that now her master had gone to Samaria to seek out the Prophet Elisha. Her mistress turned toward her.

"You know, I am beginning to believe in your God. I have never enjoyed worshipping our gods, golden statues that are lifeless." Sitting down in her chair, she began to eat. "I always thought that there was someone greater who made the earth and the stars, the people and the animals." She looked away into the distance before saying:"Your coming here, your obvious faith in spite of being captured, taken away from home, has reinforced that belief." Roza's heart was racing. "We must wait and pray now," said her Ba'alah. "The master will be away for quite a while, and when he returns then we shall know how it has gone for him." She folded her hands and Roza left her. It was all in God's hands now. She could do nothing more, but as her mistress had said, she must pray.

As Naaman left his house with the soldiers who were accompanying him, he wondered if he was foolish. Going off to seek healing from an unknown Prophet on the whim of a captive slave girl? His thoughts were troubled.

Naaman had been raised in a military family; his father had been a very powerful commander in the Syrian army. Constant war with Israel and other nations had taken its toll on him and eventually he had been slain in battle. By that time Naaman was a young man, the eldest son in a family of five and he was expected to follow in his father's footsteps. His reputation grew after he had led his troops into battle and won many victories. Given honour and riches by the king, he had acquired land and a grand house. His wife had been given to him but he grew to love her dearly. Then disaster had struck almost as soon as they were married. Capturing many prisoners, he had brought them back to be slaves in Syria. One of them had leprosy, unknown to Naaman. This man had come into his house and the disease appeared soon after. Too late, the man was sent away to a leper colony. Naaman noticed his skin lesions soon after and went to a physician. He was told that if he had children, they would be infected; his wife was also at risk. Therefore he and his wife had to live separate lives. They dwelt in the same property but Naaman slept outside in a small building on his own. They still loved each other and did not want to be parted, but it was not a proper marriage. He could not even touch her intimately because of fear that she would be infected. Often he had noticed his soldiers giving him looks, talking amongst themselves, shrinking from close contact. His leprosy was so obvious, the marks and the pitting on his arms. At night he would try and scrub his skin, hoping that somehow he could rub off the awful disease. When he had an audience with the king, he was not allowed within three cubits of him. If it had not been for his brilliance as a commander, his life would have been a lonely existence apart somewhere. Depression came at times like a black cloud. Now, after several years, he was pursuing a vague hope brought to him by this little girl. He had noticed her at the Slave market. There was something about her. Maybe she was the sort of daughter he would have liked. Her fear had touched him. That is why he had bought her to his home.

Naaman's thoughts turned to the Prophet. He had heard of him. One incident was imbedded in his mind. A troop of soldiers had been sent to capture the Prophet when he lived in Dothan. This was because it had been found out that this man had been telling the king of Israel exactly what the Syrian army was about to do. How he knew it was not known. This prevented surprise attacks on Israel. When the troops arrived they surrounded the Prophet's house. A young servant had seen them and rushed in to tell Elisha, in horror. The story went that all the troops had been struck with blindness! Elisha pretended to be an ally and led them to Samaria where he prayed for their blindness to go. However, instead of slaughtering them, the Israelites had wined and dined the invaders and sent them home in disgrace. After that shame, attacks were suspended for a while! If nothing else, this Prophet had power. Would he use it to help Naaman? That was what they would find out soon.

That night, they camped by the border of Israel posting lookouts all night. Some of the soldiers loved Naaman, others were not so sure of him.

"What a waste of time this is!" one moaned. "It is a wild goose chase."

"Oh be quiet!" another said. "If it cures Naaman then I am glad to come."

"Prophets and kings," said someone else. "Who needs any of them!"

"I would rather be chasing those pretty girls in Israel than going on a healing trip!" said another man. They settled down eventually, muttering and cursing.

Next morning, they crossed the border and reached the king of Israel's palace. Naaman had a letter for the king requesting help. Entering the palace, he was taken into the private quarters of the king.

"I have come to ask you for help," he said.

"Keep your distance," warned the king. "I do not want your

leprosy!" Naaman gave him the letter he had brought from the king of Israel.

After studying it he became enraged.

"How dare he ask me to heal your leprosy!" he shouted. "Am I God?" He stood up. "This is a plot to start a war," he said to Naaman. "He wants an excuse to stir up trouble!" He started strutting around in a fury.

"No, my Lord," said Naaman. "I have a slave girl who told me about the Prophet Elisha. He does miracles and we were hoping he could cure me."

"Rubbish!" said the king."That so called Prophet is a madman!"

In the court was a servant who knew Elisha well. Slipping off, he ran to the Prophet's house and told him about the rumpus going on in the palace.

"Who is this man," asked Elisha.

"He is the Syrian commander, he has leprosy and heard of you through a slave girl that he captured from Israel," said the young man. "He seems desperate for help."

"Tell the king to send this leper to me," said Elisha.

Outside the palace, the troops were waiting to see what was about to happen.

"I told you," said one. "Nothing but trouble will come from this!"

"Get ready to fight," said another. "If they try and take us, jump on them."

That moment, the servant who had gone to Elisha returned. He entered the palace and bowed before the king.

"My king, Elisha sent a message to say that he will help this man if you send him to his house."

"Yes, get rid of these troublemakers," said the king waving his hand in their direction. "I don't want any more to do with them!"

Naaman was escorted out of the palace. It was a few miles to the Prophet's house. The young servant showed them the way.

"I cannot wait to see him," exclaimed Naaman. "He is supposed to be a great man."

On arrival, they all gathered outside the simple, clay and wattle house.

The door opened. Naaman held his breath in excitement. A young man came out. He had a staff in his hand; he was dressed in a dark blue coat and had a short beard. He looked at them with a sullen expression on his face.

"My name is Gehazi," he said. "I am Elisha's servant." He scowled at them.

"The prophet says that you must go and dip yourself seven times in the River Jordan," he told Naaman. "Then you will be healed!" Turning, he went back into the house.

Hearing these words Naaman was shocked, then furious.

"Is that it?" he raged. "What an insult! I am a commander of the Syrian army. I have travelled for two days just to be told to take a bath! He didn't even come and see me himself; this miserable servant comes out instead!"

He turned his horse around. "Come on," he commanded. "There are better rivers in Syria than this dirty mud bath. I am not going to be treated like a slave! This journey is obviously a waste of time!"

The troops were dismayed. Naaman's second in command approached his master.

"Sir," he said. "If the Prophet had come out and asked you to do something more acceptable, would you have done it?"

"Yes of course!" ranted Naaman. "He didn't come out though!"

"Well, he has told you to do this simple thing instead," said the soldier. "Is it not worth a try? You do want to be healed of your leprosy don't you?"

Naaman hesitated. It was true. He had built up a picture of what would happen, imagined the glory of it all. Disappointment had made him angry.

He thought of his wife, then the little maid, waiting for his return with great hope.

"You are right," he said. "What harm can it do to follow his orders?"

They rode to the banks of the River Jordan. It was a dirty brown colour with bits of mud floating on the surface. Naaman felt repulsed at the thought of bathing in it. However he got off his horse, stripped off his top clothes and entered the water. He dipped under the muddy lukewarm water. Once, twice, three times and so on up to the sixth time.

"Nothing is happening," he called.

"The Prophet said seven times, sir," called his officer.

Naaman went under again. On surfacing, he felt a violent tingling in his skin. Alarmed, he looked down at his arms. What he saw was unbelievable. The skin lesions had disappeared! Baby like skin had replaced them.

"Oh!" he shouted. "Oh look!" He was amazed. It had worked! Elisha's God had healed him! It was unbelievable!

The soldiers cheered and danced, even the sceptics. Naaman came out of the river and again felt his arms, examining every patch where the leprosy had been.

"God of Elisha, I praise You," he prayed for the first time.

"Thank You." He felt that he now believed in a God who was real, greater than the gods that he worshipped at home in the temple. He must get to know more about this God and whether He lived in Syria too.

"We must return to the Prophet and thank him," he commanded. "He was right and I needed to humble myself."

So back they went to that simple house and this time the Prophet himself came out. Naaman bowed to him.

"Do not worship me," said Elisha. "Worship the God who made the heavens and the earth, He healed you. He loves you as He does everyone."

They talked for a long time; Elisha telling Naaman all about the God that he knew little about.

"Can I give you the presents that I brought with me?" asked Naaman. "Here is silver, gold, and clothes."

"I want nothing from you," Elisha told him. "Your healing is reward enough."

"May I then take two loads of earth home with me? I will put it under the tree in my garden to remind me of the God who I now want to worship. Only may God forgive me when I have to go into the temple of the king's god when he requires it of me."

"Go in peace, my son," said Elisha. "Pray for peace between our two nations."

"Thank you," Naaman grasped the Prophet's hands and wept tears of joy.

He knew that this was going to change his whole life, the relationship with his wife; the possibility of children; the end of seeing the look of rejection in the eyes of his king or his troops.

He decided not to go back to the king of Israel; his attitude had not been helpful! He would journey home with the thrill of seeing the reactions of his wife and others urging him on. As the day was drawing to a close the decision was taken to camp inside the border. Tomorrow the triumphal return to his people would begin.

CHAPTER **NINE**

Gehazi's Story and Judgement

Gehazi, Elisha's servant, was a young man aged twenty five. He had been brought up in a poor area of Israel, his family scraping an existence from the land near Samaria. One day he had been travelling to the market where he hoped to sell some produce. He came across a man who was fairly old and seemed to be struggling along. Normally he would have ignored him as he did not care much for other people but something about this figure captured his attention.

"Can I help you sir?" he asked. The old man looked up at him in surprise.

"Where are you going young man?" he inquired.

"To the market," replied Gehazi.

"Well, I suppose it would help my old legs!" smiled the man. "Thank you."

Gehazi helped him into the wagon and made room for the old man beside him. Suddenly he had a sense that he knew who this person was.

"You do not happen to be the Prophet? The man we have heard of who does amazing miracles?" he asked tentatively.

"I am him indeed!" laughed Elisha, for that is who he was. "It is God who does the miracles, I am His servant."

Gehazi did not say much more during the journey. He was unsure of what to say in the presence of the holy man.

After a while the Prophet spoke. "Tell me something about your life," he said.

He listened in silence as Gehazi told him about his existence in the small village where he lived. Eventually they reached the market town. After helping Elisha down from the wagon, Gehazi bid him farewell and they parted company.

His produce sold, he headed back home forgetting about his meeting with the Prophet. About a month later he was working in the fields, helping his father to put up fences. Their few goats had been wandering off and they could not afford to lose them. Suddenly they saw the Prophet approaching them.

"Good day sir," called his father.

"Blessings, my son," replied Elisha. He rested for a moment on a nearby seat.

"Is your visit to do with business, or how can we help you?" asked Gehazi curiosity seizing him. He recalled his previous meeting with the Prophet on the way to market.

"It is business," Elisha smiled. "I would like you, Gehazi, to become my servant. You were kind to me once, and I need help in my work for God."

Gehazi stared in astonishment.

"Me?" he gasped. "Work for you?" His surprise was soon

replaced by his usual thoughts of money. "How much will you pay me?"

Elisha threw back his head and roared with laughter. "My dear boy, I have no money. I depend on God for all my needs, and have never been in want. You will get good food, lodgings, and clothes, plus the honour of being a servant of Elisha, the Prophet." Gehazi blinked and thought hard. His ambitions went beyond being a servant to an old man who, privately, he considered slightly mad. Then he thought of the fame it would bring him. Maybe he could learn to do miracles too! People would look up to him then!

"If you really want me, then I will become your servant," he said. "What does my father say?" He looked up at his father who had said nothing yet.

"I would count it an honour for one of my sons to be your servant sir," his father said. "My younger son can take over Gehazi's duties, he is old enough now. When do you want him to start?"

"As soon as possible," replied Elisha. "Next week when the sun has risen, come to my house and I will be waiting for you." With that he turned and walked away. Gehazi's head was reeling. To get away from this God forsaken plot of dust, to a life that might turn out to be a lot more exciting appealed to him. He could hardly wait.

Elisha knew about Gehazi's desire for status; his greed for money. However, he believed that this young man needed a change of lifestyle. This, he felt, might change him into a godly man. He would train Gehazi; speak to him of God and His ways. Everyone deserved a chance to change. Thus Gehazi came to live with Elisha and his training began. It was a simple life; shelter, food and clothing were provided. He had to learn to obey Elisha and respect him. Whatever he was asked to do, the expectancy was that he would carry out the orders. Grudgingly he complied because he really believed that it would bring him fame. He would bide his time; maybe the old man would die and he would take over.

One day they went to Shunem, where a woman who was greatly regarded in the town offered them hospitality. When they returned there on another occasion, she showed them a small room on the roof of her house.

"I would like you to use this place whenever your journey brings you here," she said. Elisha was very grateful.

"Thank you." He bowed to her. "It is just what I need."

Every time they travelled that way, this room was their resting place. One day Elisha called the woman.

"What can I do for you to repay the kindness you have shown me?" he asked.

"I am well," she replied. Gehazi had noticed something.

"She has no child," he told the Prophet. "Her husband is too old to give her children."

"Call her back," commanded Elisha. When she returned, he said "You will have a child by this time next year."

"No, my lord, do not mock me!" she cried.

"I never tell lies," Elisha smiled at her. "You will be blessed beyond measure."

It happened as the Prophet said. Great delight filled that house as a son was born to the woman. Time passed. One day Elisha was out in the fields with Gehazi. They saw the woman running towards them. "Ask her if all is well," Elisha ordered. Gehazi went to meet her.

"All is well," she told him but carried on until she reached Elisha. She fell at his feet. "I told you not to mock me," she wept.

Gehazi roughly tried to push her away.

"Leave her! Run to the house and lay my staff on the face of the young lad. He has been struck down." Elisha said.

"My chance of fame!" exclaimed Gehazi to himself. "I will raise this boy from the dead. Everyone will hear of it!" He ran as fast as he could, tore up the stairs of the house to where they had laid the boy. He laid the staff on the lad's face and waited. Nothing happened. After a while, bitter disappointment filled Gehazi's heart. Miracles apparently did not favour him. By then the woman and Elisha had arrived.

"Leave me alone with the boy." Elisha ordered them all out. Several hours passed. Gehazi was in a bad mood. Why had he not been able to raise the boy? Then the door opened upstairs. Out came the boy, a beaming smile on his face. Elisha followed. He came up to the woman who was looking as if she had seen a ghost. "Here is your son," he pushed the lad toward her.

"My Lord!" she fell at his feet. "Thank you."

"Go in peace," Elisha said. "God has plans for this boy; it is not his time to die yet!"

On the way home Gehazi was fuming inside. He hated Elisha for the way he had treated him. Pushing him away when all he was trying to do was stop this woman from humiliating the Prophet! Sending him on a futile mission to lay the staff on the boy, knowing it would not heal the lad. His heart was black that day. The change of heart that Elisha had hoped for in him was not evident yet.

A few years passed. Gehazi was now settled in his role as Elisha's servant. He was aware that Elisha was trying to train him in godly ways; he pretended to go along with it for he did not want to return to his family. In his heart though, he wanted that status and recognition from others. A bit more money would be good too.

Then came the day when a troop of soldiers and a great commander came to see the Prophet. Elisha had been told of trouble at the palace; the king was very angry because of a letter sent from Syria's king asking him to heal his army official who had leprosy. Summoning the visitors, the Prophet told Gehazi to go out to them with a message. He did as he was told. "Rotten foreigners," he grumbled to himself. "Why should they be healed?" He was not impressed with the appearance of Naaman. He was covered with skin blemishes. He delivered the message and then went back inside. Through the window he saw Naaman's reaction and was amused. The commander had obviously expected Elisha to come out, not him. However, he was more interested in the wagon load of clothes and what looked like money bags. He would like some of those things! Later, there was a stir outside again. Elisha went to see what it was all about although he knew exactly what had happened. Gehazi was staggered. The Commander's skin was a clean as a baby's. He had been healed! Joining his master, he listened to the conversation. Naaman was overjoyed and was thanking the Prophet with tears. Gehazi was horrified when he heard Elisha refusing to receive a reward from all the good things in the wagon. His heart sunk. There would be no new clothes or money coming their way. As he watched the visitors leave, he hatched a plot to lay his hands on some of that treasure. Pretending to fetch water from the well, he waited a while then mounted his donkey and sped after Naaman. He was seen and when he reached the visitors Naaman got down from the wagon.

"Is all well?" he asked the servant.

"Yes, all is good," said Gehazi. "Only, two sons of the prophets have just arrived at our house. They need clothes and if you could spare a talent of gold-----?" he hesitated, aware of what he was doing.

"Of course," said Naaman. "Have two bags of money and two changes of clothes."

"Thank you kind sir," beamed Gehazi.

"Two of my men will carry them for you," offered Naaman.

When they got to the hill before the road went down to the house, Gehazi took the spoil and thanked the soldiers. He ran quickly to the back of the property where he could hide his treasure. Then slowly he ambled through the door and greeted Elisha.

"Where did you go Gehazi?" asked the Prophet.

"To get water, my lord," replied the young man innocently.

"Did my heart not go with you my child when you ran after Naaman to lie and cheat him out of his goods?" Elisha's eyes bore into Gehazi's nonchalant expression.

"No, you are wrong!" shouted Gehazi.

"I took you on hoping that living with me would change you into a man of God. I have failed. Your heart is black; the leprosy that Naaman was healed of will be with you and your offspring forever!" Elisha pointed to the door.

Shock overwhelmed Gehazi as he saw a whiteness creeping over his body.

Screaming in fury he ran out of the house and disappeared from Elisha's sight. He was never seen again in that area. The Prophet later heard that he was living in a leper colony many miles away.

CHAPTER TEN

A Desperate Wait for News

Roza's daily routine dragged on as she and her mistress waited for Naaman's return. It had been two weeks now since he and his troops had left for Israel.

"If only we could hear some news," complained the Ba'alah. "I cannot settle to anything."

"It is in God's hands," whispered Roza. She too was wondering what could be happening over in Israel. Life was quiet without so many soldiers marching outside the house; only the guards were around. Deborah, in the kitchen, and the other servants, were restless too.

"The mistress hardly eats anything these days," said Sarah. "She is growing a bit too thin for my liking."

"My supplies order has gone down," remarked Lydia. "Those soldiers used to eat such a lot!"

Waking each morning, Roza prayed that a miracle healing had taken place for Naaman. "If only he could come back healed," she wished with all her heart.

On a beautiful day, just after sunrise, Roza got up as usual and dressed the Ba'alah, served her breakfast before having her own. Suddenly she heard hooves and shouts coming from outside the window. Jumping up from her seat, she dashed to see what all the commotion was about. There, before her, was Naaman's company. The Ba'alah was already outside. She was standing, motionless, with her hands up to her face. Roza followed her gaze. She started to shake, and then tears flowed down her face like a waterfall.

Walking towards them was Naaman, hands held out to his wife. His skin was pink and clear. He looked like a young man full of vigour and new life. His wife ran to him and they held each other as if they never wanted to let go.

"Oh, oh!" cried Roza. "It has happened! The master is healed!"

The other servants were also gazing in wonder at this scene.

"Well, God be praised!" said Sarah. "Your faith has been rewarded Roza!"

"I will have to triple the order. Those soldiers will be starving no doubt!" Lydia laughed out loud.

"Back to all day cooking!" chortled Deborah.

"Best of all, the master will be able to be a proper husband to his wife," said Jacob the man who worked in the fields. He had come in for his breakfast just as the soldiers arrived. A captured Israelite, he had grown to love Naaman just as most of the other slaves had.

Roza was not called to see her Ba'alah all day. She cleaned, cooked and sewed, her heart beating so fast that she thought it would burst. There was a lot going on in the house. Furniture was being moved, beds going upstairs, stairs being cleaned; a general upheaval. None of the servants were told what it was all about; they could only guess.

"The master is moving in, I expect," said Sarah. "They are making his rooms ready."

That evening all the servants were summoned into the main entrance hall.

The master and the mistress came downstairs to speak to them.

"As you can see," announced Naaman, his face shining, "I am well again. Thanks to the God who I now worship, my leprosy is gone. I had to obey the Prophet Elisha's orders which were to bathe in the River Jordan. It is a miracle!"

"Everything has changed," the Ba'alah was smiling. "The master and I will both live in this house. Your duties remain the same but you will have to get used to his presence. Some of the idols will disappear from the courtyard. The large tree in the centre of the garden will be a special shrine to the God who healed my husband. He is the God who made the heavens and the earth, a living God, not a dumb idol. Hopefully this house will be a lot happier for us all." She dismissed them and signalled for Roza to follow her into the tapestry room. Roza, her heart still thumping, obeyed. On entering she was told to sit on the stool at her Ba'alah's feet. Naaman came in and stood behind his wife as she sat in her chair.

"Roza, we are eternally grateful to you," said the Ba'alah. "Your courage and lack of bitterness, your faith and willingness to speak to us about the Prophet Elisha have brought healing and renewal to us."

Naaman came round from behind the chair.

"Young maid," he gently murmured. "The day I saw you,

I knew you had special qualities. God meant you to come here. He has used your courage and faith to bring salvation to this family. Thank you."

Roza bowed low. She could not say anything. Her feelings overwhelmed her and she knew that if she tried to speak floods of tears would embarrass her and them.

"Go and rest now," said her Ba'alah, "Tomorrow is a new day!"

In her bedroom, Roza knelt by her mattress. "Thank You my Father," she breathed. "Your will be done for the rest of my life."

Sleep did not come easily; she was too excited. Her dreams when she did sleep were full of light.

The next morning when she went to the Ba'alah's room she noticed a change. A door in the right hand wall that had been sealed up was now obviously in use. It had brightly coloured hangings and a silver handle on the door.

"The master sleeps in there," said her mistress. "He has his own special servant to look after him." She looked radiant. "How old are you now Roza?" she inquired.

"Fifteen, Ba'alah," replied Roza. "I have been here for two years."

"Old enough to get married," the mistress laughed. Then she stopped as Roza looked so sad. Roza remembered that she was not supposed to show her feelings and was a little fearful.

"Why so sad?" she was asked.

"There was a boy called Daniel," Roza took a deep breath. "He was my best friend but I don't know what happened to him."

"When you were captured, did anything bad happen to him?"

"I do not know. The last time I saw him he was lying on the ground having been knocked down by one of my captors," replied Roza.

"I would have married him."

The mistress said nothing, and Roza washed and dressed her before going down to the kitchen to prepare breakfast. Her thoughts drifted to her homeland. Would she ever know about her family? Tears pricked her eyelids but she pushed them away and concentrated on what she was doing. She was valued here now; God had used her in an amazing way. She must trust Him. That day, Naaman resumed his duties with the soldiers. There was a new atmosphere in the house; melancholy had been replaced with cheerfulness. Most servants had a history of having been captured and bought to this place. Only Sarah was Syrian, she had been the Ba'alah's childhood nurse and had come with her when the mistress had married. The others had adapted to life here and seemed content in their duties. Some had married other slaves and lived nearby in small huts. Their children were hardly ever seen as they were sent to outlying schools and when home lived away from the main house. The only unhappy servant was Hannah who worked in the garden. One day, encountering her, Roza asked her what she thought of Naaman's healing.

"It does not change anything for me," said Hannah. "I still hate them all."

Roza plucked up courage. "If you could only forget the past and accept your life here, happiness might be possible," she said timidly.

"How can I?" Hannah scowled. "My life could have been so different!"

"God can help you to forget Hannah." Roza tried to put her arm around Hannah but she pulled away.

"Why did he allow me to be captured; my family to be murdered?"

"I do not know," said Roza. "My parents may be dead too."

"Well, you are very popular here!" snorted Hannah. "No one takes any notice of me!"

"Maybe they see your anger and are afraid to speak to you? I was at first."

"One day I will escape from here. I am planning it now," Hannah smiled. "They will not miss me. I don't expect them to run after me." She glared at Roza, "You dare to tell anyone; I'll make you sorry!"

Roza sighed. "Your secret is safe with me Hannah. I will pray for you."

There was nothing more to say. Hannah's bitterness had poisoned her so much that it was hard to see her changing. Sometimes, she realised, you have to leave people in God's hands.

One morning when dressing her Ba'alah, Roza noticed that she had put on weight. Her clothes were difficult to get on her.

"I am finding it hard to do up the fastenings Ba'alah," she said shyly.

"Roza. I am going to have a child," her mistress told her. Roza gasped and her eyes sparkled.

"I never thought this could happen." The Ba'alah's eyes filled with tears. "God has given me a chance of great joy."

The news soon spread through the household. Everyone was excited.

"Well!" said Sarah. "I am not too old to be a nurse again!"

"Another mouth to feed," said Deborah the cook. "I expect this will be the start of other children! They have waited long enough!"

Roza wondered if this would change things for her. She had experience with looking after children; she had nursed her brothers.

The Ba'alah would probably want her own nurse. She could only wait and see.

A loud cry woke Roza. She jumped out of her bed and opened the door. Upstairs there was a commotion. Washing herself, she dressed and went to the stairs. Sarah was coming down looking flustered.

"They have called for the midwife," she exclaimed, "the child is coming!"

"Shall I go to my mistress?" Roza asked.

"Not today child," said Sarah, "leave her to us. Go and have your breakfast and wait for instructions."

Roza obeyed feeling very excited. She would clean and do any sewing until called. As she was cleaning the stairs, Naaman rushed in. He dashed past her and tried to go into his wife. The midwife told him quite firmly to go away and all would be well! Looking downcast and very anxious, he came down the stairs, barely glanced at Roza and went outside again. She could see him pacing up and down until one of the soldiers ushered him away.

The day passed. Occasionally screams of anguish drifted through the house. At twilight a most welcome sound reached the ears of the servants. A baby's wail! Sarah wrung her hands together in joy. "At last!" she cried. "It has been a hard labour." She went upstairs with more hot water and blankets.

Coming down again she announced: "It is a boy! A healthy, beautiful boy!" Everyone shed a few tears of joy. It had been an eventful day.

"Someone go and tell Naaman," commanded Sarah. It was not long before he came rushing in. That evening great celebrations took place. A house that at one time had been gloomy and dark was now filled with the sounds of laughter and rejoicing.

CHAPTER **ELEVEN**

Amazing Happenings

Roza's routine now included helping her Ba'alah with the new arrival. She looked forward to the mornings when she would dress the mistress, then help her to feed and wash the baby boy. His name had not yet been chosen; in Syrian culture it was very important to decide on the right one. It took a while for Naaman's wife to recover from the birth. The master was in and out of the house obviously thrilled with his son.

One day news came into the kitchen, where the servants were eating, of Hannah the girl who worked in the garden.

"She has run away," announced Sarah. Roza tried not to blush. Hannah had told her of this plan a while ago.

"What will happen now?" asked Lydia. "Will they go after her?"

"The troops have been told to scour the area," Sarah replied. Roza wondered why they were bothering as Hannah had been a sulky unfriendly servant. She prayed that Hannah would get away. The girl had been so unhappy here.

Nothing more was said for a few days. Then she was told that Hannah's body had been discovered washed up on the river bank not far away. She had been trying to cross to the other side but had drowned, overcome by the strong current. Everyone was very upset. Roza shed tears over Hannah. She had never been able to forgive her enemies; her life had been filled with bitterness. "May she be at peace now dear Father," she prayed.

The baby boy was named Yakob Naaman. He grew strong and healthy, a delight to all. Often the mistress would take him into the garden and she could be heard singing to him. Her life was now so much happier; Naaman too was prospering. One day a Syrian woman arrived. She would do a lot of the caring for Yakob as was the tradition. Roza was not sure how this would affect her duties. Her life was about to take a change of direction in a way that she could never have imagined.

It was about two weeks later when she was summoned to attend to her Ba'alah in the downstairs sitting room. Mystified, Roza went into the tapestry room. There, Naaman and her Ba'alah were waiting.

"Roza, we have something to talk to you about," said Naaman. Roza stiffened in fear. "What now?" she thought to herself.

"We have decided to release you," the Ba'alah said. Roza stared at them.

"I do not understand," she falteringly whispered.

"You have been here three years or more," Naaman smiled. "You have brought great blessing to our lives by your courage and faith. We want you to have a better life, one that will be among your people."

"I do not know if my family are still alive," Roza said.

"We have decided to send you to the Prophet Elisha; he will find out about what happened to them."

"How will I get there?" asked Roza.

"I myself will take you." Naaman reassured her. Roza could not help herself. Tears ran down her cheeks.

"I have been happy here," she sobbed. "You have treated me kindly."

"It is not the best future for you living here," said the Ba'alah. "You need to marry well and be blessed in your own land. I want that for you."

Roza felt weak with emotion. It was a shock to be told this; she would need time to get used to the idea of freedom. They dismissed her and she went to Sarah. Telling her about the news was like sharing it with a mother. Sarah hugged her and held her for a while.

"God bless you my dear child," she said, "your future is in His hands; maybe this is His perfect plan for you. You have been faithful to Him, now your reward will come."

"Suppose my family are dead?" cried Roza.

"You will never know unless you go and search for them." Sarah touched her cheek, "we will miss you. Light has come into this house because of what you have said and done."

So it was settled. A month later Roza packed her few belongings and was put in the wagon beside Naaman. Everyone, including little Yakob, stood and waved her goodbye. Tears were on everyone's face. For the first time Roza found out that her Ba'alah's name was Delilah. The mistress enveloped her in her arms, a thing normally unheard of, and told Roza quietly that another child was to be born soon. The sense of being torn in two came over Roza. She longed for home, but loved her captors. Waving until the wagon turned the corner, she prayed a blessing on those who had been a part of her life for so long. Looking ahead at the mountains she whispered: "I lift my eyes to the hills. Where does my help come from? My help comes from the Lord who made heaven and earth."

CHAPTER TWELVE

A Future Unknown

It was a long journey to the Prophet's house. Roza slept a lot. They stopped for refreshment half way. Naaman took good care of her. Two other soldiers had accompanied them on horses.

"Are you alright child?" Naaman asked.

"Yes my Lord," replied Roza, "but I am a little scared."

"All will be well," Naaman smiled at her. "I am sure of it."

Eventually they spotted the small house which had smoke curling out of the chimney. "We are here." Naaman dismounted and helped her down from the seat in the wagon. The door opened and Elisha came out. Roza had never met him before. He was an old man with a greyish beard. Stooped, he used a staff for support. His eyes were what caught Roza's attention. Piercing brown, they penetrated her soul. His cloak was hooded, brown in colour.

"Welcome Roza," he greeted her. "I have heard about you. It seems that you have been talking about me with good results!"

Roza blushed. "My Lord," she bowed low. "Can you help me find my family, if they are still alive?"

"Are you prepared for sadness as well as joy?" the Prophet asked.

"I can only leave it in God's hands," replied Roza.

"Good girl. That is the right way to look at things," Elisha beamed.

They were ushered into the small house. It was warm and cosy inside. Upstairs there was one room, downstairs was open with several areas set apart for cooking, washing, and sitting. Food was brought out by a servant who was young looking and quietly spoken. After they had eaten, Roza was shown to a bed upstairs. She washed and lay down. Soon she knew nothing, exhausted after the journey. Waking in the morning light, she slipped to the floor and prayed earnestly that her family would still be alive, especially Daniel. "Your will be done Father God," she breathed. Sitting on the bed she wondered what the next few days and weeks would bring her. Going downstairs, she saw that Naaman and the soldiers had departed.

"They thought it best," Elisha said to her. "You have already experienced too many goodbyes." He motioned for her to sit at the table. Breakfast was bread, curds, and honey, warm milk was her drink. "We have to go to Thirza today and see what we can discover." Roza's heart started to beat quickly.

Dread, mingled with excitement filled her. She looked down at her feet.

"What is troubling you child?" asked the Prophet.

"It was my fault that I got captured," said Roza. "I was disobedient to my parents and went into the fields alone."

"Alone?" Elisha's piercing eyes searched her face.

"No sir, I was meeting Daniel my friend." Roza reddened.

"Ah!" No more was said for a while. "We shall go and see what has happened." The Prophet went outside and saddled two donkeys. Roza followed. "Can you ride one of these?" she was asked.

"Yes, I think so." Roza was not sure, but it did not look too hard.

Together they got onto the donkeys and set off toward Thirza. Roza soon found that riding a donkey was possible as long as she held on tightly, especially over the bumps! The gentle animal seemed to sense that she was not used to riding him. He went slowly and stopped every so often as if to check that Roza was alright. They rested for a while under a huge tree and had some food. By mid afternoon, the landmarks were becoming familiar to Roza. Fear and apprehension filled her when they got to the fields surrounding the village where she had been born. When they got to the well they dismounted and watered the donkeys.

"What shall we do now?" asked Roza.

"We will go to the centre of the village and find the Elders. They can help us to discover news of your family." Elisha laid his hand on Roza's shoulder.

This was the moment that she had dreaded; she could not bear it if the news was bad. Hesitating, she almost wished that she was back in Naaman's house but she knew it was wrong to think like that. Fear was not trusting God; she must believe that He was in control. Taking a deep breath, she followed Elisha toward the village square.

Three elderly men, dressed in black robes looked up as Elisha and Roza approached. They were sitting on a bench outside the meeting place in the sunshine. Recognizing Elisha they stood up and bowed.

"My father, you are welcome," they said. Gazing at Roza, one of them gasped.

"Is it you my child, is it really Roza?"

"It is me teacher," answered Roza not really recognizing the man.

"Where have you been?" he asked.

"I was captured and taken to Syria where I have been serving as a maid to a man named Naaman," she replied.

"Did you run away?"

"No. God used me to tell my master about Elisha. He had leprosy. Because of my faith he went to see Elisha and was healed miraculously. Then he let me go; he took me to Elisha out of gratitude for what had happened to him. Are my family still alive?"

"Sit down Roza." A place was made for her on the bench. She realized that she was shaking.

One of the other men started to speak.

"On the day of that raid three years or so ago," he started, "your four brothers were in school here. When we realized what was happening, I took all the boys down into the cellar below the meeting place, where we hid. It was terrible. We could hear the screams and sounds of destruction above us. Suddenly we heard footsteps coming down toward us. The door to the cellar opened, and two bandits came down. We were discovered. They looked at us for a moment. Then they separated the younger boys from the older ones.

Grabbing those poor older boys, they took them upstairs. I followed, pleading with them to let the boys go. All I got was a kick to my head and I remembered no more. When I awoke I was in the meeting place on a mattress. The younger boys and my brother elders were around me. Roza, your two older brothers were taken away. I believe they are in Syria too, where you were taken.

I know no more than that. Your two younger brothers are still here in the village."

"What of my parents?" asked Roza as her tears started to flow.

"Roza. Your father was in a meeting with other elders. They were in a house at the end of the village. That house was set on fire and they could not get out. I am so sorry Roza. However, your mother was in the fields. She hid herself among the trees near to where she was working. Hearing all the noise, she wanted to run and see what was happening. Good that she did not! Terror was in her heart no doubt. After it was all over, she crept back to the village in the dark. Poor woman! She found out that her two older sons were gone and you too had been captured. Her husband was dead. Grief has changed her, Roza. She is here, but is ill. Many others in Thirza suffered in the same way losing sons and husbands. As a community we are helping each other but the wounds are still raw."

"Daniel, my friend who I was with when the raid came, what of him?" whimpered Roza.

"You mean Daniel, Hiram's son?" asked the Elder.

"Yes, he and I were with the flocks out in the fields," Roza said. "He was knocked out by the bandits and I was captured. The last I saw of him he was lying unconscious on the ground."

"He is still alive," said the Elder. "They thought he was dead so left him, but he was not. All the flocks were stolen though. His father escaped and went looking for him. Daniel has moved away, not far, where he is now training to be a carpenter and a house builder. He is good with his hands."

"Is he married?" asked Roza urgently.

"No, not yet," smiled the Elder. "He has never forgotten you Roza. He keeps talking of going to find you in Syria. Other girls have tried to woo him, but they get nowhere."

"Will my older brothers ever come back?" Roza wept freely now.

"There are plans to send the soldiers secretly to Syria to search for the boys that were captured. Women too were taken."

"I know," said Roza. "I was with them. We were sold in the Slave Market. Some of the women were probably married off to Syrian men."

There was silence for a while. Roza felt overwhelmed with grief for her father and her brothers. Guilt filled her. She should have been there. What could she have done though?

Elisha stood up and gently raised Roza to her feet.

"We must go to your mother Roza," he told her. "She needs to see you; the fact that you are alive will be a comfort to her." He turned to the Elders.

"Will you show us the way?" he asked.

"Does she still live in our old house?" asked Roza.

"No Roza. Your father's brother built her a new house nearer the centre of Thirza. He is the closest relative and has redeemed her and the boys. They are not married because your mother is not well enough but he is her legal Kinsman. He is kind so you will be alright with him around."

The walk to where Roza's mother lived was agonizing for Roza. How would her mother greet her? Would she be angry, blaming Roza for what had occurred? It was about ten minutes away from the village square.

Stopping at the gate, Roza looked at the house. It was bigger than her original home. Made of stone it had a staircase at both sides of the house. The windows on the upper floor were evidence of several rooms. On the lower floor it looked as if there was lots of space, the door stood ajar so she could see inside. Then stairs went down to a basement area. The courtyard was large with a small well in the centre. Pots of flowers stood at either side of the door. There was no sign of life.

Suddenly, two figures appeared in the doorway. A bit taller, sturdier than she remembered them, it was her two younger brothers. As it was a Sabbath day they had not gone to school. They stared at her.

"Matthias, Benjamin, I am Roza, come back to you," she called. Behind them another figure appeared. It was her mother. Pushing the boys aside, she walked toward Roza. Her face was drawn and pale. Grey hair framed her head below the veil that she was wearing. She seemed to stagger a couple of times as if not too steady on her feet. When she got to Roza, she gazed at her as if looking at a ghost.

"My daughter, is it really you?" she wept tearfully.

"It is I mother, come home to care for you," Roza reached out for her mother.

"I am so sorry for disobeying you and not being with the boys when I should have been." She then told her mother exactly what had happened those three long years ago. Her mother clung to Roza for a long time.

"Samuel and Nathan are in Syria," she said. "We have heard nothing from them. Your father is dead."

"I know," said Roza. "The Elders told me all about the events of that dreadful day. Can we go inside please and I will tell you of all that God has done in my life whilst in captivity." So they went inside where food was prepared and Roza was shown around the new house.

"Your uncle is looking after us now Roza," her mother told her. "I am not able to marry him yet; when I get well maybe then we will be man and wife. He is a bit older than your father but he is so kind and patient. You will like him."

"Does he know about me?" asked Roza. "Will he be expecting me to live here and help you?"

"Yes, I told him all about you and how you were captured by the Syrians."

"Will you forgive me for that day mother?" pleaded Roza.

"I forgave you long ago Roza. Nothing would have changed what happened that day. It was probably better that you were out of the village. Perhaps you would have been killed."

Over the next few hours Roza told her mother every detail of her capture and how God had arranged for her to tell Naaman's wife about Elisha. The healing of Naaman; the joy of a renewed marriage; a child born and her release out of gratitude.

"It was almost like Joseph being taken to Egypt in the old stories," she said. "He was used to save the lives of his brothers and Jacob. I feel that God wanted Naaman to be healed and for him to come to faith. He sent me there to bring them hope."

Her mother took this all in. "If only your father had not been killed and Nathan and Samuel taken away." She looked so sad and old that Roza grabbed her hands.

"God can bring the boys home again," she sobbed. "Father has gone to be with God. We can ask Elisha to look for them, Naaman will help I am sure. He feels indebted to Elisha."

Elisha had gone to visit other people whose sons and daughters had been killed or kidnapped. Roza found him later that day. He was resting in the shade by the village well.

"Father, can you help find my older brothers in Syria?" Roza asked timidly.

"I would need help," replied the Prophet.

"Naaman might be willing to search for them. He goes everywhere with his soldiers," Roza looked eagerly at Elisha.

"I will ask him Roza. He is so grateful to you. I will also send my servant to ask around the villages and towns. He likes to be active."

"Thank you." Roza bowed down and the Prophet touched her fondly.

"I am going back now," said Elisha. "If there is any hope you will hear in due time."

Roza, restored to her family, settled into her new life. Her uncle accepted her into the household willingly. She helped with the daily tasks and continued to care for the boys. They were more capable by now and did a lot of the outside work. All the time Roza's thoughts were turned to Daniel. Did he know she had returned home? Would he come and see her? It was not a woman's place to seek out a man. It had to come from him. She hoped and prayed for a reunion.

CHAPTER **THIRTEEN**
Young Lovers Find Blissful Happiness

Daniel nursed his throbbing hand. He had just hit it accidently with a hammer while making a cupboard. His friends working with him were laughing.

"Your mind is not on the job Daniel," one mocked. "Thinking of a girl?"

"Yes actually," Daniel retorted wincing in pain. "She is called Roza and I have heard a rumour that she has come back to Thirza after three years away."

"Why was she away so long?" he was asked.

"She was kidnapped by the Syrians who left me for dead. We were together when they came. I have always prayed that I would see her again somehow." Daniel shifted his weight from one foot to the other. He was feeling unsettled and concentrating on work was difficult.

"Well you had better go and find out if what you have heard is true," one of his friends whose name was Silas suggested. He was already married and knew what it was like to be in love. Marriages in Israel were usually arranged by the parents, but often the children were allowed a say if they really wanted a particular girl.

"I am going to as soon as I can." Daniel wanted to go that day but he knew that would be foolish. He would have to wait until there was a right time; when he had no other distractions or jobs to spoil things. That time came at the end of the week when work was forbidden because of the Sabbath. Setting off early in the morning, Daniel rode his young donkey towards Thirza. It was not a long journey, but he decided to take it slowly.

His mind was in turmoil. Would he find Roza? Had she forgotten him? She might possibly be betrothed to some other man. Nearing the village he hesitated. The house Roza had lived in before was no more. Where did she live now? As he looked around, he saw a small boy gathering wood from the forest that he knew so well. It was here that Roza had been running from her enemies before he was knocked out.

"Hi there," he called. "Do you know where a girl named Roza lives?" The boy stared at him.

"Who are you?" he asked.

"I am Daniel son of Hiram," Daniel replied. "I knew Roza three years ago. I am her friend."

"Well, I am her brother," the boy smiled at Daniel. "She lives just down there, by that big tree." He pointed to further down the hill where a big Sycamore tree towered over a house.

"Thank you. What is your name?" asked Daniel.

"I am Benjamin," the boy replied. He stooped down to continue picking up wood. Daniel cautiously approached the house by the tree. In the courtyard, drawing water from a small well was a young woman with her back to him. She was singing as she worked. Daniel knew instantly that it was Roza.

"Roza," he called softly. She turned round slowly. Their eyes met. For a long moment they studied each other. Roza saw a Daniel who was taller, broader, still very handsome, and whose eyes were alight with joy. Daniel saw her as a beautiful, well formed slightly older Roza. Her experiences had not spoilt her looks. Light radiated from her eyes; her dreams were coming true. Her lover was before her.

"Daniel," she whispered. He got off his mount and went to her. Moving to the side of the house they embraced, kissed for the first time. It was magical. They had loved each other from childhood. Now sixteen, Daniel nearly seventeen, they knew that they could not be parted again.

"If your mother and father are in favour, will you marry me?" asked Daniel.

"Since, as you know, my father is dead, my uncle is my guardian now," whispered Roza. "You must ask him for my hand."

"I am going to be able to earn my own money soon. Then I will build a house for us; it will be a special place just for you and me," said Daniel.

Months passed. Daniel was introduced to Roza's family who soon loved him. Roza's uncle gave permission for them to be married; the wedding would take place early next year. Daniel had already chosen a piece of land for their house. His father had given it to him as his inheritance. The only shadow over those days was the fact that Samuel and Nathan, Roza's brothers were still in Syria and no news had come from Elisha about their whereabouts.

Winter had arrived in Thirza. The cold air made the villagers stay inside their houses a lot more. Work still went on of course, but evenings around the well were scarce as it was too cold to sit there for long. One day as Roza was walking near the Meeting House she heard horses approaching. Cowering by a tree, the memories of capture still affecting her, she waited to see who was coming. Out of the mist came a crowd of horsemen led by a familiar figure. It was Naaman with several soldiers. Elisha was there too on his donkey.

They dismounted.

"Roza," called Naaman. "Do you remember me?"

"Of course, my Lord," Roza bowed.

"I have bought some people who belong to you," Naaman stood aside as two figures came into view. Staring, hardly breathing, Roza saw two boys striding toward her. It was Samuel and Nathan, older but still her boys.

"Oh, my brothers," Roza dashed forward to embrace them. They laughed and held her to them.

"Elisha the Prophet found us, and Naaman asked the king of Syria to release us along with the other captured boys," Samuel said. He pointed to behind him. Other boys were appearing. It was a day of utter rejoicing in the village. A great feast was held with Naaman and Elisha as the guests of honour.

"How are you Roza?" asked Naaman when they had a chance to speak.

"I am to be married next year," Roza said shyly. "I found Daniel, he was still alive. He is building us a house to live in," she added proudly.

"My wife Delilah has had another son," Naaman told her. "Yakob is two years old now; Darius is a few months old."

"I am glad," Roza beamed.

Roza's mother recovered much of her health after the two boys returned from Syria. At the end of the year she was married to Roza's uncle Nathaniel. They seemed very happy.

When Roza's wedding day arrived, heaven came to earth.

It was a beautiful day; the flowers decorating the Meeting House filled the air with perfume. Daniel and Roza went through the Jewish ceremony, then a week of feasting began. Their house was finished, set on a hill overlooking the valley. It was a tribute to Daniel's skill. The happy couple were escorted there by the crowds as tradition dictated. As the door closed behind them cheers erupted. Everyone felt that it was like a fairytale come true. Out of captivity and sadness, two people had triumphed and proved that God always works everything together for good, however long it takes. Faith in Him is the only requirement. Years later Roza sat with her children by the village well and told them the wonderful story of how God had taken her to a strange land to help an army commander find healing, restoration and faith in the living God. It was a tale that would be handed down from generation to generation and written in the history books of Thirza for all to read.

THE END